Sex and God

Fleassy Malay

For the incredible creatures who entered
me so deeply,
I bled you out in poetry.

contents

Your Virgin Breath- 9
Morning Ache - 10
Kissing Rocks - 13
Northern Lights - 14
Sweet Chardonnay - 18
Hunger for Harmony - 21
Born of Rhyme - 23
Only Then - 25
Be Kissed - 28
Yaku Ginger - 29
The Night I Dance with
Stephen - 34
The Wolf - 36
Sex Scenes - 39
The Night we had a Babysitter -40
The kissing of front-loaders - 42
It's Not You - 43
Laser - 45
Hidden Places - 46
An Acorn on my Pillow - 47
Butterfly Wings - 48
Longing - 49
Somehow - 51
Longitude - 53

Bleed - 54

The Spin - 55

Alone - 58

Dance Revelation - 59

Fantasy - 60

Alive - 62

Stranger - 63

After the Date - 64

Leave Me - 65

Ananda Sunset - 66

Remember - 67

"I wanted to compile *Sex and God* to allow a part of myself to be truly seen. These two subjects are very dear to my heart and are intrinsically united in many ways. To share with you my Erotic, my Devotional, and all of my grey areas in between is to show a very deep part of myself. The longing and the surrender of a queer, spiritual, sexual mother a million miles from home.

As a Spoken Word poet, I can rely a lot on my body and voice to convey the depth of my words. The act of publishing my work (including many previously unreleased pieces) in written format is an act of deep vulnerability. Not only are the topics of *Sex and God* deeply raw but the act of leaving my words to the minds and eyes of strangers, without my voice, is a vulnerable and scary thing. Yet I am never truly living when I am not leaning into these beautifully uncomfortable spaces. I hope you enjoy my words."

Fleassy Malay

Your Virgin Breath

Again You wake me
Your silent beckoning
In these early hours
When sleep has me in its arms.

Yet the sound of You breaking,
Your timid crack
Inspires my lids to open
Has me enthralled
For one small moment.

Just long enough to see your finest light

Your Virgin Breath

Before I joyfully roll away from you
Tired of your teasing

Yes
I too am excited for this day

But not yet

Let me dream a little longer.

Morning Ache

I woke up this morning
With that old familiar ache.

The yearning that begins in my guts
Musters up strength at my pubis
And runs its way down my thighs.

I woke up this morning
With that old familiar yearning.
For slender fingers
Lace, filigree and bone.

For lips, thighs, labia
And gentle caresses of the hair.
For the fire that lays
In the sentimental gaze
Of those who run with wolves and beasts.
Those who greet the sunrise
With willing breath and ecstasy.

It's been many years since I knew rest
Upon the breast
Of a woman.
Since my heart beat in time
With another's gently uttered rhymes.
With another's moon rhythms
Blood dripping

Juice Dripping
Lips Kissing

Woman with woman.
Leg with Leg.
Eye to Eye.
Eye.
Get.
You.

Got.
You.

Was.
You.

Lost.
You.

Eye.
Want.
You.

I rise and breathe deep once more
The blissful sensation of desire.
The timid moan of craving.
Let her rest in me, noticed.

Seen.
An old familiar ache.

Welcome Home.

Kissing Rocks

If I were to give myself
a moment with you
alone
I am sure I would fall
in love.

I see you
kissing rocks
in the early hours
as tender as if
they were
a child

And I know
when I am not looking
you do the same
to me.

Northern Lights

"Is that it?" You said
As I closed my book having read
Shaking guts
A poem of my hunger for you.

"Is that it?"
The air of expectancy
I mean, what did you expect from me?
I HAD said it was erotic... and It was...
Kinda.

I mean I didn't say how I had imagined
Tracing the curves of your body
With my finger tips
As I caressed
My own

But, you know
That shit's hard to say
In a poem.

Especially to a woman.
To a woman I like
To a woman I've not even held hands with
Yet Danced with
A million times in my imagination.

That shit's hard to say
In a poem.

And no, I didn't mention
In such forward words within the verse
how my body responds to you
How the warm, wet, pulsating song
Of my vagina
Sings out
like...
...like...
...like a fucking siren into the night.

Because, well

I'm afraid of being the one left dashed upon the rocks
Left weeping in the arms of my partner
As he lovingly holds me
Through yet another wave
Of my pain.
Again.

And yeah... I would have liked to have told you
how I sometimes conjure up your smile
In my mind
as my body writhes on lonely nights.

How your music makes my spine arch.

How sometimes I use your face
To take me
Over the edge.
I lay in bed
Ashamed
I never asked your permission
To lay you across the skies of my imagination
And make love to you
Like Northern Lights
On a winters night
In Alaska.

I didn't tell you
How I often think
Of buying you flowers
But don't,
Out of respect for your fiance
You share such a beautiful, bold and tender love
And though everyone's in
The know
I dunno...
That type of courage
Escapes me.

And maybe...
Maybe one day
I'll find a poetic way
To say

"Woman.
I am drawn to you like oceans to the moon.
I long to lay upon your shores
Touch my fuzzy cheek to yours
To share bed with you
Break bread with you
Moonlight walk, deep talk
And give head with you"

But you know...

That shit's hard to say
In a Poem.

Sweet Chardonnay

I lay amongst the vines
Drunk on wine
Made from grapes grown in this very soil.

My body cries "Halasana!"
But I do not move...

Limbs limp from Chardonnay and from not so far away
An accordion plays
As guests dance golden in the light of the setting sun.

The hills of the Yara valley
Scorched yellow in the heat,
Dy spikes of grass
And gumtrees house the Cackle Crack of the kookaburras
laugh...

But I lie amongst the rows of Pinot and Merlot,
Rich green and watered with care,
Each row a potential hiding ground for inspired lovers to
entwine
And I let my mind
Take me there.

I recline.
Baddha Konasana
Soles of my feet together
Knees marking East and West.
The wind lifting my skirt across my mid drift
And it's here I let my mind play

Let a shadow fall upon my face
There, ruffle haired stranger is placed

Today?

Eyes green like the vineyard leaves...
Or blue like this southern summer sky...

A smile

A touch

And kisses crush plump grapes as we drink the sweet
wine of a lovers embrace
We allow fingers to frame foreign fruits and let juices
satiate the parched earth,

A drunken sort of Yoga as we bend and breathe...
Intoxicated by the greatest spirit around.

A sound in the distance of laughter,
A light breeze brings me to vague sobriety.
The Bride prepares to make her speech

Again I am alone amongst the vines,
Drunk on wine
And a little taken by the sweet nectar of my mind.

Time to return to the wedding parade... join the jolly guests
And possibly test
Another glass of that
Sweet Chardonnay.

Hunger for Harmony

This desperate desire I have
To fall deeply
In song
With someone.

There is some indescribable force
Which exists in my bones
That knows peace only
When my voice meets another's.

When two notes
Drift so close
That they become one.

Or when the space between
Is just far enough
that Waaa   waa   wa   wa wa wawawa
Waaaaaaaaaah

Harmony Happens.

A split second of surrender
My soul dies for a moment
and all that exists
Is this dance
Of reverberation.

Suddenly all matter is singing

And I am one single note
In a symphony of sound.

I ache
It physically hurts
This desire to entwine
To find a voice
To sit beside mine.

I

I hunger

I hunger for harmony
And every day I close my eyes
And listen intently
To this lonely tone
Which is mine.

Born of Rhyme

There are days
When music makes me
My feet are pounding
Rhythms on concrete
And beats perforate my soul.

There are days
When music
Licks at my heels
In time to the furious rays
Of Summer.
In time to the tempo
Of elation
Which bubbles in my guts
For the knowing
That dark days are past.
At last.
That my head and my heart
Are moving in time.
That Harmony grinds
its way through my pain
And I'm moving with a symphony
Orchestrated beyond me.
That I am but one beautiful note
In and epic crescendo
Of Love
Which rings it's way

Silently throughout history
And continues to reverberate
Beyond my being
My time.

Born of Rhyme.

I'm
Made
of Music.

So dance with me.

Only Then

When I say "I want to dance with you"...what I mean is

"I want to Dance with you"

To know my own movements, through and through
And then (and only then)
To turn to you.
Make contact and move.

Slowly at first, just your hand with mine, find that divine
Timing between to and fro
I lead, I follow, I lead, I follow

I lead... I follow

Until neither of us is sure who is leading who.
It's just one movement shared between two...
Then (and only then)
We kiss.

Our lips skipping beats yet always on time, perhaps your
Fingers through my hair, perhaps not
Either way my focus would stay on that point where your
Lips are touching mine,
Or your hand is touching mine
Or if it is that our legs meet

Our thighs entwined to the curious beat of our passion;
Our knees touching for a moment just to know the touch of
The others
And resting here our eyes meet as lovers...
Then this for me is fine.
Our Dance could be a dance of the eyes,
Where the penetration is the gift of your gaze.

Our Dance could rest here and we would be complete.

Then again, movement could take us elsewhere...
You would have no need to push me on the bed
For I would already be there
With you
Before we even knew that this is how we would move.

Your masculinity would be evident
In how you held
My gaze.
Your strength... a mirror to my own.

We would bend to each other carving pathways to Ecstasy
Then (and only then)
You enter me.
When I can see my strength in your eyes.
Then (and only then)
Will it be right.

And we shall dance all day and all night
...In fact it will never end
As lovers or friends...
From then on every Breath is a Kiss...
Every Movement ... a Dance.
Dancing together whether together or apart.

This is what I mean
When I ask you
To Dance.

Be Kissed

"Let me kiss you" he said
So I raised my head
Lips to meet his
His weight above me
His chest the sky
I raised my head
Lips to meet his.

"Stop it"
he said
"Let me kiss you, Let yourself be kissed"

He graced my face
With tender placed gifts
Of appreciation.

"Just let yourself be kissed"

Yaku Ginger

The rain pounds down outside
A tropical twist to this mist covered land
Where rocks and trees
Bring grown men to their knees.

The thunder rolls in
Lightning strikes
Flirting with the life
Of ancient plants
This is the land where the Kami dance.
Where all life begins and ends
And the mountains decide
Who shall survive
And who shall fall to fertile earth
Top soil soft with rot
Moss carpets cover rock
And green is the only spectrum
To be seen.

I hide from the damp kiss of the mist
In a wooden hut built in a way
That rocks jut up between floor boards
And in central place
In solid grace
Grows a tree.
Reminding me
I'm only as hidden as I perceive myself to be.

Because this forest is built
Of eyes.

Between branch and bough
Are the webs best blessed
With God's with eight legs
Waiting patiently and playing melodies
On threads
That only we can hear.
And who are we
To fear these musical God's
That mark protection to our path.

I bow my head and ask permission
To pass safely through these lands
Clap my hands
Clang clack on the bell rope
Rat-Tat money in the hatch.
But my prayers do not rest here

They follow me deep into the jungle amongst the trees
Where the Kami
Rest upon the leaves
And I leave
All I have been trained to believe
About religion
And it's basis on greed.
And stories of the beginning of time

And who's versions have enough proof
To prove theirs is right.

Because to me
That's just playing games with the divine.

And here in my cedar church
Bare-feet wet with oriental earth
The details of faith
Hold no base with me
My interest in intricacies
Lay in what's surrounding me
My religion?
Simplicity.

And here beneath the watch of the sky
It's hard to deny
There is something bigger than me.
But surely
A Prayer is a Prayer
Who ever receives.
And to meditate
By any other name
Would smell just and sweet
And inner peace
Is inner peace
No matter the name of the road
You choose to receive.

And me?

Well I guess my Bible
Is built of Earth and Stone
And the words are written
In a code
Complied of Flesh and Bone
And So

Here, within this cedar church
Bare-feet wet with oriental earth
I bow my head before the great
Sugi Tree
It's wisdom and it's strength lay
In it's three thousand years
It's roots hold together
History.

I am on my knees
Before the centipedes
A butterfly
Sparrow sized
Flutters by
And I cast my prayers into the air
(To what ever is there)

"Gratitude and thanks
For my days here.

Thanks and praise
For all the places I have been
All the things I have seen
All the visions in my dreams.
Gratitude and thanks
For my friends
And my family."

But of course
The forest pays no mind to me
Just carries on
With it's whistle-song of a thousand years
After all I am not the first
To cast my prayers here.

I rise.

The thunder and lightning long past
The rain now a damp cloud
Around
The mountain peak.
I head home
And with one last glance
I bid farewell to the land
Where the Kami
Dance.

The Night I Danced
With Stephen

Last night
He lifted me skyward
Raised my body as if it were barely there.
Raised my body skyward
And let me fall.

You came to my mind
As close eyed I plummeted towards the floor
Face first
Your chest the sky
Face first
I the earth
Face first
He caught me inches from the ground.

I had barely flinched
Or drawn breath
The whole way down
As if I were barely there.

It was here
The music and he
Had full control

I surrendered
As I have to you a hundred times.
Always aware there may be a drop
But prepared to make it a dive
From great height.

He rolled me
Across his knee
To my feet
And I drew my head to his chest
rested my hand on his heart
Knew the lover in him
That I know in you

With him
It is dance
Lovers of the Wave.

With you
It is dance
Lovers of the Ocean.

The Wolf

I writhe
Head bent to the night.
My spine arched
I search the dark
For the glimmer in your eye.

We
Entwined.

Your Sweat
My Thighs
All Wet
All Grind.

I Pant.

Gently humming the song of my arousal.
You
Grunting.
We
Sing.
Out of tune
Out of time

But who gives a fuck

Because right now
The only beat I can hear
Is the Pounding of my heart
Matched
With the Pounding of the bed
Matched
With the Pounding of Pelvis into Pelvis
The Pounding of Pleasure
Into Pain
Into Pain
Into ecstatic Pain
Into Pleasure again.

My Nails
Your Back
My Skin
Your Teeth

We
Grit and Bone
We
Coarse and groan

Words slipping from my mouth
(Words my feminist resists...
But words that slip so easily out)
"FUCK ME"
I am screaming

Your grunting
Strangely appealing

We
Bulge and contract
Appear and react
Until puddles form around me
Wet succulence surrounds me
I am only me
I am no longer me
I am beyond me
I cave inwards
Burst outwards
And fall back upon the pillow.

Strangely tired now.
Strangely quiet now.

Your limbs grow tree-like around me
We fold in together
And darkness prevails.

Sex Scenes

"Disturbed People create
Disturbed sex scenes"
Says the lady in red trousers
Loudly to everyone who listens
As she shuffles through the train carriage.

The Night we had a Babysitter

I close my eyes
Let my skin do the seeing
As you paint patterns on my form.

Ropes bind my need to control
Yet my mouth is left free
To yell boundaries
And desires
As they
Rise.

My Eyes
Closed
My Breath
Heaving.

The gentle hum of your arousal
Met by the rhythm of my writhing.

We have Been distant.
We have Been close.
And there were times
When we almost were not Being at all.

Then there are times like
This.
Times when Being too melts away
And all we are
Is Fire
Flesh
And Fornication.

The Kissing of Front-loaders

There are moments
Between the kissing
Of front-loaders and concrete.
Between the singing
Of reversing diggers
And mothers with health issues.

Moments where your silence
Creeps in
Relieving
It all.

The wind
Caresses my cheeks
And your greatness
Becomes the backdrop
To my day.

It is not you

The grip
Of your fist
Tight around throat
Leaves me gasping
For more
Than just
Air.

My hair
Tangled in tightly bound
Knots.
My body
Pinned against yours.
This moment
Just before I cum

Where time stands still

And all I am
Is bated breath and bone
And even you don't exist
Despite
Your heavy weight
And my constricted air ways.

Despite
Your penetrating gaze.
Despite
The utterings under your breath
I am left
Gasping
For the split second
I get
To see
God.

Laser

"I'll buy you a laser"
You say
"And I'll write tales of our love
on the moon".

Hidden Places

How sweet it is
What exists
Within the hidden places.

An Acorn on my Pillow

Once he gave me an acorn
With two green leaves
He said he was turning his own over
Changing colours to keep me.

But fear
Always took me
And the road
Always calls.
And the day I left for Russia
All I could recall
Was his smile
The way he held me.
True.
How he would wake me
When I was sleeping
Just to whisper
"I love You".

From St Petersburg
To Tokyo
I rambled
And I roamed
But every night
When I laid my head
I'd always dream
Of Home.

Butterfly Wings

99 wings upon my bed
In a gesture of things
That were left unsaid
And instead of holding
We let them leave
But I cling to the wings
In a box beside my dreams.

And stoned
He rode
his bike off in the dark
I gripped my hair
As if it were my heart
Took a deep breath
And lay my head to the sand
And touched my face
To this foreign land.

The season for sailing
Or the season to stay
These are the shores
Of lovers washed away.

Longing

The trees here don't know my name
And I wonder if you
Still let it slip between your teeth
At night.

I'm sure I'm fine
It's just
As much as I don't want to
I miss your life in mine.

I forget to look at the stars now
I hide away in bedrooms
Escaping adventure
Dreaming of a loving touch
But hoping no wandering eyes
Stray my way.

It's too soon to be with someone new
But too long since I knew you
and desires just leave me confused.

Daily I'm fine,
I walk in long grass and listen
To the crickets song
Engulf myself with other people's stories

After being sick of my own
For so long.

But tonight I wish
It wasn't some other traveler
Who will be returning to my room
Sharing prices to make life cheaper

I wish tonight,
For once,
It was you.

We would forgive each other
Like we always do
And just lie
With my head on your chest
Sharing the songs of insects outside.

You would stroke my hair
And comment on how long it has got
And I would kiss your stomach.

But it is never going to happen
And when the door opens
It never is
You.

Somehow

When I walk these streets
Heavy-hearted
You are there.
In the cracks through concrete
Your hope shoots through
Like resilient weeds
Reclaiming the streets
Of my aching heart.

When "Too Much!" thunders through
My skies
And my rage burns
Flecked with lightning strikes
Of unearthed shame.
In the deafening silence
After the storm.
You are there
Uttering a gentle reminder
To breathe.

I notice you most
In these moments
When the story feels too twisted
Complex
For my tiny perspective.
And I wish, for a moment,
It would all end

So all I see
Is you
Ebbing in the Silence.

But of course it doesn't
And when I wake
In the space
Between
The rattled cage
Of a toddler's patience
And the boiling of the kettle.
Between
The cracking walls
And bowing floorboards
Where sunlight and mosquitoes
Creep in.
Between
heavy hearted steps
And the joyous tangles
Of post-coital hair.

In the cold moment
Between
Bed and shower
Autumn and Spring
Broken heart and warm arms
Somehow
Despite my ignorance, You are there.

Longitude

This longitude
Stirs my Attitude
I long for you
Across Latitudes

Why make this world so large?

Bleed

When Something in you Cracks
and you Bleed
Poetry.

The Spin

There are days when apathy becomes me.
Like a fire burning to see the light
I'm blinded by my own desire
Left lying awake at night
Afraid of things that might come,
Afraid of one thing or the other...
My mind is Spinning.

Anxiety has never been a friend of mine
So "Why" I ask "Do I still invite him to share my bed?"

Keep these thoughts whirling in my head?
Round and round and now I see
Why the Sufis do it...

They knew it had potential
To Spin beyond their own mind,
Catch it up and leave it way behind so all that's left
Is the nothingness of all, God's call
A silent prayer in the night while lights and traffic keep at it
And a baby cries in the distance
In this instance all there is is the Spin.

So I try it myself but I'm left helpless
Because my room's too small.

Arm stretched and like Alice I'm looking for something to make me smaller.

It's a tall order in these days
When everyone wants to expand
Grow Bigger
Buy More
Upgrade and Download
Knowledge on our iPhone
So we know
We'll die
Content.

But like a wrench in the works all it does is make it worse.

So still I need to clear my mind
Pull my arms down to the side
Or up to the sky
To make space for this
This Spin.

If the only way to beat my brain is to let my heart over take

Then take me.
Break me
Make me the ember of your love
Take the very core of me

Take all of me so all I see is You
You in how the trees grow
You in how the cities go on all night
You in light and darkness
Spinning
You in the end of my mind
Spinning
You in the darkness of these hours when I lay awake,
Spinning
You at the end of it all
Afters tears, torn, tatters for all
I'm Spinning

Spinning until colours merge and words hold no meaning
Neck bent and screaming to the night
(To the neighbours' delight)
Spinning
Bouncing off the walls
Until all of them fade
and all I see is the Spin.

All I see is the Spin
And in that
Nothing.

Nothing
And
You.

Alone

Alone
I wake
And crave
The shape
I can not
Make
Alone

Dance Revelation

You do not need
To be involved in story
You soar Golden and Strong
You shine the light of God all around
and
Fuck
You can
Dance.

Fantasy

And I think of you
And wonder
If it is right
To put a face to these feelings.

To imagine your skin
Brushed against my thighs
Your moisture on my lips.
To create a scenario
Which may never arise.

I think of you
As if you wanted me
As if we wanted
Each other
For a moment
And I let my body moan
To the tender tune
Of music you have never
Composed.
All for the sake
Of living out
An exotic fantasy
Completely fashioned
From ungraspable concepts.

Your lips
My lips
Your hands
My hands
Your body moving
Closer
And I wonder
If it is right
To put a face
To these feelings.

Alive

I come alive
In those moments
Between unknown
And known,
When the void
Is filled
With the intoxicating
Scent
Of another's
Curiosity.

Stranger

We have never touched
Skin unfamiliar
Yet her laughter has left
My labia engorged
Her sidewards glances
Left chances
For my body
To respond.

Even in those silent moments
Between notes
I have felt my body ache
For something I don't know

And for a split second
I surrender
Into the idea
That we are already lovers
And time forgot us
Long enough
For us
To make mischief
Of the evening
And a mess
Of each other's
Hair.

After the Date

"If it's not God, I'm not interested"
She said to herself
As she avalanched inside
And sky became dust
And dust became a gourmet moment.

As God wrapped
Herself
Around
Herself
And wept
For everything which is
And is not
Simultaneously
God
Or
Something
Half as deserving
Of her aching
And surrender.

Leave Me

Leave me in the arms of my lover
Bother me not
with your stories and rhyme
For I'm
Taken
With Their touch upon my skin
and They are busy
Making music of my soul.

Leave me in the arms of my lover
Do not blow wind in my pipes
For they are already singing.
Do not divert my gaze
For They're all I need to see.

Leave me in the arms of my lover
Or better yet
Lay in them with me.

Ananda Sunset

Sitting at Ananda watching the sun
Play passive games with the sea
"I'll only come to you
If you come to me"
All the while edging closer
Unseen
Until he mounts the mountains
And paints the sky with his Pink Passion
By which time
It's too late to decide
And he lays back
Under the covers of darkness
To play the same games
On other lands
Ripples dance with the thrill
Of his touch
Light lighting faces
Fallen upon the scene
Breath stolen by the setting
Of dreams
Golden puddles
In my eyes.

Remember

So it is
Here
In my heartache
That I finally
Remember
Your
Face.

About the Author

Fleassy Malay is a Spoken Word poet from the UK now residing in Melbourne Australia. She runs one of Melbourne's most acclaimed Spoken Word events, Mother Tongue, and has spent the past 4 years dedicated to the empowerment of Women's voices in this space. She has been performing for over 20 years, writing poetry for 15 years and performing Spoken Word for 10. After her studies at The BRIT School of Performance Art and Brighton University she found her passion for the authentic voice in performance through poetry and Spoken Word. Her life-changing course, Speak Up, has been running for 4 years helping people step up with vulnerability and authenticity to be seen more fully in this world.

She has performed internationally at gigs, festivals, corporate events and award ceremonies as well as facilitating workshops and classes for all ages. With multiple recordings, albums and a children's book under her wing, *Sex and God* is her first collection of written poetry to be
published.

Printed in Australia
AUHW011927120820
332391AU00002B/29

9 780994 490513